DINO WARS

The Trials of Terror

DAN METCALF

illustrated by **Aaron Blecha**

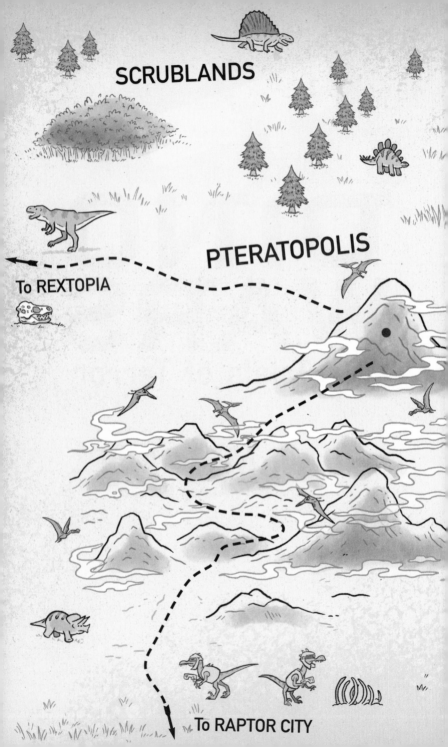

MARSHLANDS

Old Lund

Chapter One.

"Twenty-three green bottles hanging on a wall… twenty-three green bottles hanging on a wall…"

Adam puffed as he walked up the narrow mountain path. The ground underfoot was rocky and the slightest misjudged step could spell disaster. He had to concentrate each time he placed his feet down or he could easily find himself sliding down the mountainside. The mountain itself was man-made, comprising of the rubbish and junk from a thousand years of waste. Adam remembered his dad telling him that they used to bury rubbish in the ground but when that filled up, they kept piling it up high, until they needed flying machines to dump more on the top. After that, they dumped rock and gravel over it, called it a mountain and pretended that it was their plan all along. Adam found it easier not to speak. Instead he focused on his breathing; the higher up they got, the thinner the air became and the harder it was to take in a breath. *Goodness knows how Benji and Tuppence manage to keep singing*, he thought. He wouldn't have minded their cheerful tunes if they hadn't chosen to start with nine hundred and ninety-nine green bottles…

"And if one green bottle… should accidentally fall… (puff, puff, gasp!)… there'll be twenty-two green bottles hanging on a wall!" The twins sang happily, their curly brown hair bobbing along.

Behind them, four tiny dinosaurs trotted along on their chicken-like legs. They followed the twins wherever they went and were similarly unaffected by the walk that the group had been on for nearly two days now. The lycorhinuses were simple creatures and could only manage a word each.

"GREEN!"
"BOTTLE!"
"GREEN!"
"BOTTLE!" they chimed.

"Please can I pick the next song?" asked Chloe. Adam's sister trailed behind him, swigging from a water flask. She was as tired as Adam but, as he had not yet suggested they rest, she did not want to either.

"Nope! I've got dibs on 'If You're Happy and You Know It'," laughed Adam. Chloe rolled her eyes. Behind her a large iguanodon crept along, using his large feet and his front claws to pick his way up the precarious path. Dag was strong so despite carrying with him a collection of his cherished tools and inventions, his breathing was normal.

"As long as it isn't 'The Grand Old Duke of York'," he said. "I've heard enough about walking up hills…"

The final dinosaur bringing up the rear was Oska, an oviraptor. Even though his thin body and his scaly legs were made for running, he was wheezing constantly.

"Can I vote for silence?" he asked. He was the oldest of the group of travellers and was unused to exercise. "I'm finding it rather tricky to walk with all this noise."

"Cheer up, Grandad!" called Tuppence, from the front of the group. "I reckon we're nearly there! Maybe another half a day of walking?"

"Anyway, it's only walking forwards. But, you know, up," said Benji. He leapt forward, almost skipping up the path. He was as light as a mountain goat on his feet and just as fearless. Adam's heart skipped a beat when he saw Benji nudge a small rock over the side of the path. It tumbled down the steep mountainside and cracked into two pieces at the bottom.

"Easy for you to say, young Benjamin!" said Oska. "You have younger legs than some of us!"

Benji stopped and turned.

"What, these old things?" he joked. He jumped up and down on the spot in a sort of jig, demonstrating his youth and litheness. The rest of the travelling party laughed, but in his jolliness Benji had taken his eyes off the ground. He slipped on a piece of slate and his leg went from under him.

"Benji!" screamed Tuppence. She reached out to grab him but it was too late; he fell on his front and slid off the path, down the slope beside them and out of reach. He did not scream, but scrambled to grab onto something – *anything* – that might stop his fall.

Adam and Chloe ran forward to help – amazingly not tripping themselves – and Dag followed.

Benji saw his friends drifting out of view as he slid down the mountainside, but he had not given up on rescuing himself. He spied a weed to his side sticking out of the sharp rocks and grabbed it. It slowed his fall and he stopped, desperately clinging to the plant. Looking down, he saw a sharp drop just metres away. He had found the plant in the nick of time but he had no clue how long it could hold his weight. Even as he lay on his front with a drop to certain death below him, he managed to glance up to his friends and give a cheeky smile.

"Um, a little help?" he yelled.

The gang leapt into action, all eager to get their friend back on the path. Adam leaned down and tried to reach him, but he could not get anywhere near him. The lycorhinuses, Grak, Trek, Karp and Hart, held each other by their feet to make a chain of dinosaurs, but they could not get close either. Tuppence was in shock; she could do nothing but shake and scream insults at her brother, which at least kept him distracted

from his predicament.

"You bleedin' idiot! I should've kept you on a lead like a dog!" she yelled.

"At least I don't smell like a dog, you stinkin' mongrel!" Benji called back.

"We need a way of getting him! Something secure! Come on, think!" said Chloe. Adam turned to her, his face red. His panic had turned to anger.

"Maybe instead of issuing orders, you'd like to try doing something yourself!" he snapped. "Grab my legs, I might be able to get closer."

Chloe crossed her arms.

"And who made you the big boss man?" she asked.

"At least I have an idea!"

"A stupid one! You'll end up at the bottom of the mountain yourself if you try that!"

Dag shook his head in disbelief. Even in an emergency, Adam and Chloe Caine could still find time to have an argument.

Oska finally caught up with the group.

"Can I suggest we save the arguments until later?" he said, out of breath. But the siblings carried on.

"You're always bossing me about!"

"That's 'cos someone needs to be the leader! I never–"

Dag flipped a catch on his large suit of metal armour and a small compartment opened. He took out a length of strong paracord.

"You're wasting your breath," Dag said, as Oska looked on. "Once they get going, they could argue until the next ice age. Give us a hand, will you?"

Between them, the two dinosaurs fashioned a lasso out of the paracord and threw it down to Benji, who freed up one hand to loop it around himself.

"You're not the leader here! Just 'cos you're

the one who got us into this mess!" continued Chloe.

"That's a low blow, Chloe, even for you!"

Tuppence and the lycos joined Dag and Oska in attempting to heave Benji up the slope, and soon they had successfully pulled him close to the path. Scrambling for a handhold, he reached out his hand to Adam.

"Guys – help me up!" he said. The rest of his friends were gripping onto the rope, trying not to let it slide through their hands but Adam and Chloe were still bickering, oblivious to Benji below them. "Guys?"

"Adam!" called Dag. "Chloe! Help him!"

Benji attempted to climb up higher but slipped again. The sudden jerk on the line caused it to slide through Dag's claws, and Benji fell a few metres back down the slope before Oska took the strain and stopped him.

"ADAM!" Dag yelled with all his might.

Suddenly Adam stopped arguing and he snapped back to the emergency in hand. He leaned down and pulled Benji up to the path, finally safe. Tuppence enveloped her brother in a hug and the lycos jumped on him in relief. On the path, Dag shook Oska's claw and turned to Adam and spoke in a low tone, so the twins wouldn't hear:

"We need to talk."

Chapter Two.

They paused for a while on a section of path that was wider than usual. They needed time to drink some water, to calm down and for Tuppence to stop shaking.

"Come on Tups," said Benji. "Anyone would think I'd just escaped a brush with death!" he joked. Tuppence, in no mood for jokes, punched him in the arm.

Adam sat ten or so paces from the rest of the group, legs dangling over the dangerous precipice that they had just battled against.

Dag passed Adam his bottle of water and plonked his large dinosaur butt down next to him. He didn't say anything for a few moments but just slowly rewound his paracord into a ball.

"What was all that about then?" he asked. Adam looked sheepish and could barely look at his best friend.

"I, er…" Adam was desperately looking for an excuse for exploding into an argument with his sister and nearly letting a member of their team perish on a mountainside, but anything he thought of seemed a bit… trivial. In the end, he gave up and shrugged. "I got angry."

"With Chloe?" said Dag.

"She just expects me to do everything she says, all the time! Lead the way, save the twins. Plus, she *always* has to be right… it's so infuriating! You know how she is." Dag was an only child and an orphan like Adam. He didn't have a sister but, by growing up in the peaceful settlement of Bastion with Adam and Chloe, he had come to think of them as his siblings. Dag spied a small plant on the path. He ripped it up with his bony claw and popped it in his mouth. As a herbivore, he could eat most plants, which came in handy when they were travelling. He chewed and pulled a face. "Ugh… Snow Willow. So is *that* why you're so angry with her all the time?"

Adam shrugged. Part of it was that Chloe was his sister – they had always argued, but always made up. Having no mum and dad, they had to. They had no one else. But another part of it was something that was much more recent…

"It's this quest. I never asked to be leader y'know…" he said sulkily.

"No, but you *did* volunteer to come and disarm the weapon," said Dag.

Adam nodded. He had volunteered because, deep down, he felt like it was all his fault. When he had found an ancient war bunker, *he* had insisted on going in. It was *he* who had activated the computer and *he* had set off a timer to release a bio-weapon that could kill all the dinosaurs that now roamed the earth. When Adam thought about it all, it set his heart racing and his face went red.

"We need four Dilotron crystals to disarm the lab making the virus, yes?" said Dag. He fished into a knapsack and brought out a yellow and orange crystal which glowed with energy.

"We've got two – so we're halfway there! All you have to do is keep your temper under control and we'll be back in Bastion before you know it."

"You make it sound so easy," smiled Adam. Dag shrugged.

"It's a piece of cake! A walk in the park! Like shooting fish in a barrel!" he laughed.

"Now, let's climb this mountain and break into a city full of razor-toothed, carnivorous pterosaurs!"

So they trekked onwards and up the mountain where the air grew thinner and the terrain grew trickier. Adam looked up at their destination – Pteratopolis. Perched high up on the side of the mountain, the city looked like a bird's nest that Adam had seen once on a tree back in Bastion. There seemed no way to get in from the bottom, where the team of friends would meet it, but Adam reasoned that there didn't need to be. The entire settlement was home to pterosaurs – winged dinosaurs who had no need of stairs or doors. They simply flew in over the walls. In fact, to their knowledge, no human had ever been inside the city; it remained untouched during the Dino Wars that nearly destroyed the human race. Even the map that Chloe had taken from Bastion trailed off into vague sketches when they got near to Pteratopolis.

"Come on everyone!" chirped Benji. The fall had done nothing to dampen his spirits. "Twenty-two green bottles hanging on a waaaaall!"

Adam, Dag and Chloe burst out laughing. It was an infectious giggle that even the usually serious Oska joined in on.

Suddenly Chloe stopped.

"What is it?" asked Adam. Looking out across the valley behind them, Chloe raised one hand and pointed. Adam and Dag squinted to try and make out what she was showing them. Beyond the great woods, deep in the gorge, lay Bastion, the settlement they had left a few days ago. The only thing that indicated it was there was a tiny trail of smoke, probably coming from the toolmaker's forge.

"Home," said Chloe. Dag nodded.

"We'll get back there, Chloe," said Adam. "I

promise."

Chloe turned back and wiped her eye.

"We'd better, Adam Caine," she said, pressing onwards. "We'd better."

Chapter Three.

"YEEHAH!" yelled Tuppence as they finally reached the end of the path.

"YES! WE–" began Benji, but Chloe's stern look and her finger pressed to her lips stopped him. "*–did it*?" he completed in a whisper.

"Yes, hurrah and hooray for us," said Chloe, unenthusiastically. "But we're still right next to a city full of carnivores! If they hear us they could tear us limb from limb!"

Adam stepped up to the end of the path where a wall blocked their passage. It was brown and made of large branches and even whole tree trunks that had been piled on top of

each other. *It must have taken the pterosaurs years to build*, thought Adam.

"So this is Pteratopolis," he said aloud. "What do we know about it?"

The team shrugged.

"All I know is that you don't say the 'P'," said Dag.

"If I may?" said Oska from the back of the line. "Little is known about the pterosaurs and their kind. They fought side-by-side with the raptors in the Dino Wars of course, and they were good soldiers. I remember one time we laid waste to an entire unit of the Human army when we–" Oska stopped his journey down memory lane when he suddenly remembered who he was travelling with. They stared at him, horrified by the thought of the Dino War battles. They were too young to remember the wars but they still had to live with the effects. "Ahem. Excuse me. I was saying that the pterosaurs keep themselves to themselves. Being airborne, they could build their nests up high and avoid the petty fighting after the war had ended. Pteratopolis itself, as you can see, is a fortress."

"So we know nothing about them?" said Dag.

"Well, the few times I was able to talk to one in the war, I found that they are very noble, almost regal creatures. They prefer to fish and scavenge rather than fight and attack."

Adam nodded, thinking. *Excellent*. If they were lucky, they might find that the flying dinosaurs were friendly old birds with more interest in fishing than fighting. If they were unlucky however, they might find themselves to be their dinner.

"Let's get started then," said Adam. "How are we getting in?"

The team set about searching for a way in, although Adam knew there wouldn't be any. There was no need to build doors in walls that the pterosaurs could just fly over. If they did, it would be like inviting humans and other ground-based dinosaurs into their city.

Tuppence found a small gap in the weave of logs and branches.

"I can see daylight through here!" she said. Grabbing a fallen branch, she pushed it in the hole and wiggled it about furiously. Slowly the hole grew wider. "If I can make this big enough, I can squeeze through…"

With all eyes on her, she climbed in and began to crawl forward. The mood amongst the team of friends was upbeat. Perhaps she would make it.

"Umph!" came a distressed cry from inside the wall. Tuppence's feet were poking out of the hole.

"Problem?" called Chloe.

"Um… yeah. Turns out this wall is pretty thick and I can't make it through to the other side after all. And the hole I made isn't big enough," said Tuppence. There was a note of embarrassment in her voice. "And… and I'm stuck."

While Benji lay on the floor laughing until he cried, Adam and Dag grabbed both of Tuppence's feet and pulled hard until she popped out again. Looking around, Chloe had another idea.

"It's pretty tall," she muttered, looking up. "But I reckon we could climb it. We used to climb the walls of the gorge back in Bastion, remember?"

They had often played together as young children and one of their games was to see how high they could get up the walls of the gorge that surrounded their home. Adam, the competitive one as always, would often attempt a run-up and try to leap up the rock face. Dag would use his strong claws, but his weight would always bring him down. Chloe, however, had the perfect mix of daring and cautiousness, planning and nerve.

"Give it a try," said Adam. Chloe rubbed her hands and grabbed a handhold. Heaving herself up, she quickly found her footing and was climbing up the wooden wall.

"Whoo! Go Chloe! Go Chloe!" called Benji and Tuppence, until Chloe silenced them with a look.

"This requires concentration, you know!" she called. But the distraction had been enough to make her misjudge her handhold. She grabbed a thin bit of branch which snapped and she fell. Chloe screamed, but Dag caught her in his strong dinosaur arms. "Oops! Maybe I could try again…"

Adam shook his head.

"It's too dangerous. Anyone else got an idea?"

Oska nervously walked forwards.

"Well if we can't go through it, and we can't go over it," he said. "Perhaps we could go under it?"

He scratched at the bottom of the wall and cleared some rubble out of the way. He was fast for a raptor, with his little arms scooping away the dirt. Suddenly–

CLANG!

Oska stood again, shaking his claw and muttering.

"Ouch! It's no good. There's a layer of solid metal here – could be an old automobile. We'd need more than my aged claws to get through that."

Adam, sat on the ground, looked up at the huge wall. He hadn't battled velociraptors and

scaled a mountain to be beaten by a wall. They just had to work out a way of getting through…

As the rest of the gang sat, munching away on their ever-shrinking pile of food, Dag leapt up.

"What's the matter?" asked Adam. "Did you get bitten by a fire ant?"

"I just remembered! My heli-kit!" he said. Dag excitedly ran to his metal suit of armour that he had removed in order to sit down and flipped open one of the compartments.

"Heli-kit?" repeated Adam. "Why do I think this is not going to end well?"

Dag pulled out a vest with two small metal arms attached. On the end of the two arms were rotor blades.

"Back in the times before the Dino Wars, they used to have flying machines called helicopflers," Dag began.

"I think you mean 'helicopters'," said Oska.

"Whatever. They had huge blades on top which span around to lift the machine into the air," said Dag. He was almost dancing with excitement. "So I tried to recreate it with this."

Adam watched as Dag strapped on the strange invention. He clipped it around himself and grinned.

"Dag, there is no way that thing will make you fly!" said Adam.

"Fly? Oh no! It was a complete disaster! I fell and almost broke my tail!" Dag still seemed strangely positive. "*But*: what if I sharpen these metal blades and move the arms so they face forward? They'd spin so fast I could cut through the wood! I could turn myself into a living saw mill!"

Adam paused and nodded. It could work. They could get through the wall!

"Grab some rocks!" Adam said. "Everyone get sharpening!"

Everyone joined in and picked up rocks to scrape along the blades of Dag's contraption. Soon the blades were looking shiny, sharp and, if Adam was being truthful with himself, pretty dangerous.

"Okay, stand back everyone!" Dag said. He had positioned the metal arms so they faced forward and pulled down his goggles over his eyes. With a pull of a cord on his chestplate, the rotors whirred into life; the sound was like a swarm of wasps attacking Adam's head. "HERE WE GO!"

Slowly Dag walked towards the wooden wall and the buzz of the blades suddenly got louder. Grinning with delight, he was quickly lost in a cloud of sawdust.

"IT'S WORKING!" he yelled. "IT'S WOR– UGH!"

With a cough and a splutter, Dag got a mouthful of wood shavings. He spat and tried to

clean himself up, then gave a cheery thumbs-up to Adam. "IT'S DEFINITELY WORKING!"

"Thank goodness one of his inventions finally did…" muttered Adam to himself.

PAPIER:860 mm x 610 mm OUTPUT: Magnus_K_SM5_150LPI

Chapter Four.

Inside the city of Pteratopolis the sound of Dag's whizzing rotor blades started as a hum and rose to a deafening roar. With a crash, some logs were splintered apart and Dag emerged into the sunlight of the city, covered in wood shavings and spitting out sawdust.

"Eugh!" he said. "Maybe I should bring a full face mask next time." He removed his goggles to reveal two clear, clean circles around his eyes, which looked comical next to his dusty scales.

"Next time?" said Chloe. "I'm not planning on coming here again…"

The rest of the group emerged into the city

and looked around. There was nothing on the ground apart from a few boulders and rubble, interspersed every few hundred metres with large tree trunks.

"Where is everyone?" said Benji. The entire city looked deserted. Oska looked up and cleared his throat.

"Ahem!" he said, pointing upwards. "I think we are meant to be looking up there…"

Looking up, Adam saw what Oska was talking about. The tree trunks that stood there were huge, not grown naturally but instead propped up by rocks. *The pterosaurs must have air-lifted them in by themselves*, thought Adam, *then stood them up and rolled the rocks to keep them upright*. He marvelled at how many winged dinosaurs it would have taken to lift each log, which were each carved with beautiful designs. But that wasn't the most impressive thing. Atop each colossal tree sat a gigantic nest;

the living quarters of the pterosaurs.

"That's their homes?" said Chloe.

"Yep," said Adam. "Hope you like heights..."

"What? Me? There is *no way* I am climbing up there!" said Chloe.

"I don't see any other choice," said Oska. "If you really want to locate this crystal of yours, it is most likely to be safely tucked away in the home of a leader, just like it was in Raptor City."

"You'll be fine, Chlo'," said Adam.

Chloe spun around to look at her brother with an expression that Adam recognised as the 'don't-you-speak-to-me-like-that' look.

"Why do you think I'm going to climb it?" she snapped.

"We've already established that you're the best climber!" said Adam. "Why are you making a fuss about it?"

"It's not the climbing I'm worried about! Why don't you climb into a nest full of ravenous

dinos?"

"Here we go again," muttered Benji. Dag, Oska and the twins exchanged looks. Even the lycos seemed to be weary of Adam and Chloe's arguments.

"STOP!"
"FIGHTING!"
"STOP!"
"FIGHTING!" they barked.

"I've got a new plan!" said Dag, stepping between the two of them. "Let's split up into two groups. We'll cover more ground that way. Chloe, me and Oska cover the east of the city, while Adam, Benji, Tuppence and the pipsqueaks go west."

"HEY!" snapped Karp. Grak seemed to stick out his tiny tongue at Dag, who still hadn't forgiven the lycos for attacking him

when they first met.

"Sounds good to me," Adam turned to leave so quickly that the twins had to chase after him. They were followed in turn by a line of lycorhinuses. The comical Hart brought up the rear, wobbling and zigzagging, unable to run in a straight line.

"Let's go," said Chloe, scowling and marching off in a huff.

*

Dag, Oska and Chloe headed off east as planned. The city was built on a natural plateau where the rock levelled out and the terrain was easier to walk across than the mountain path had been. There were still small, loose rocks around, but at least they didn't have to worry about slipping and

tumbling to their deaths. Chloe trudged on ahead, clearly in no mood to chat with her new group. Dag and Oska kept a few paces back in case she felt like taking out some of her anger for Adam on them.

"Have they always been like this?" asked Oska.

"Hmm? Oh, you know. They're family, so yeah, they fight now and again. And again, and again, and again!" Dag smiled. "Adam's got a short fuse and Chloe doesn't like being bossed about, so they're not a good mix, if you know what I mean!

Oska laughed and nodded.

"Ha! Yes!" he said. "Typical humans, eh?"

Dag looked over to Oska to see if he was joking or not.

"What do you mean?" he asked.

"Well, the humans are known for fighting. They battle each other, disagree over everything,

start wars…" Oska said. He wasn't smiling anymore. "You're too young to remember the Dino Wars, of course?"

"Um… yeah," said Dag. He wasn't sure he liked where this was going. "So?"

"So you don't know what *they* were like," said Oska. He had a glazed look on his face and a faraway look in his eye.

Dag walked along in silence for a minute or two. Did Oska think that because he was a dinosaur, he automatically hated humans? Dag had grown up in Bastion, where dinosaurs lived side-by-side with humans. He had never known the world that Oska had fought in. He ran forward to keep pace with Chloe.

"So… where do we look for this Dilotron crystal, then?" he asked.

"Up there somewhere I guess," she said, still half-sulking. "They don't seem to have lights, so they're not using it for electricity like we did in

Bastion."

"And there aren't any statues of mad leaders like in Raptor City," said Dag. He looked guiltily at Oska. "No offence! I know Stryker was your nephew…"

"But you're right. He was driven mad with power when he wore the crystal," said Oska. "Shame, really. He was delightful when he was small. Excellent pianist, you know…"

They arrived at one of the tall trees with the dinosaur nest on the top. Chloe looked up at it, thinking something over.

"You don't have to climb up there if you don't want to, Chlo'," said Dag.

"It's okay, Dag," she said. "I've got a better idea…"

*

Meanwhile, Adam and his group had come across their own tree. They stood at the bottom,

looking up at the huge structure.

"Big, innit?" said Tuppence. "Like, *BIG*-big."

Benji nodded. "Big," he agreed.

"BIG!" said Karp. The rest of the lycos nodded their chicken-like heads.

"You guys really need to learn some new words for 'big'," said Adam. He assessed the climb. While he wasn't as good a climber as Chloe, he was still adept at scaling large structures. Staring at the tree and its nest on the top, he wouldn't be able to attempt his usual run-up-and-leap technique, but then again, that was only fun when he was racing against Chloe. He could easily climb the rocks which propped up the huge trunks and then the tree seemed to have many foot and handholds in its trunk to scale it. Occasionally there were branches to hold on to and rest upon. Adam, looking forward to the challenge, clapped his hands together and

rubbed them. "Let's do this!"

He set about clambering over the rocks.

"Rather him than me," muttered Benji behind him. "He could break his neck..."

Adam paused slightly as he overheard Benji. If something was too dangerous for even Benji, the boy who had once eaten a thistle for a bet and who used to bait a herd of triceratops into chasing him 'just for a laugh', then maybe Adam should be thinking twice about it.

"No time," Adam said to himself. Always in the back of his mind was the ticking clock counting down to the start of the Coda Program, the set of events that would trigger the release of microspores that would kill all of dino-kind. "My fault," he muttered aloud, not meaning to.

And so he set about the difficult climb. Step by step, hold by hold, he found a rhythm and was soon three-quarters of the way up. Looking outwards, he could see the impressive view over

towards Raptor City and Bastion, but he didn't dare look down.

"Nice one, Adam!" called Tuppence.

"Yeah, you're doing really well!" said Benji.

"DON'T!"
"FALL!"
"DON'T!"
"FALL!" said the lycos.

"Thanks," said Adam. "I'll try to remember that…"

After another period of strenuous climbing, Adam reached the edge of the nest. He scrambled to the side and heaved himself over, praying that he didn't come face to face with a pterosaur.

He fell into the nest with as much grace as a dancing stegosaurus and found himself muttering "Oops, sorry," to no one in particular.

"What's up there?" yelled Tuppence from

below.

"Shut up! We're trying to be stealthy!" yelled Benji, equally as loud.

Adam looked down to see eight large, dappled eggs, nestled in a bed of leaves.

"Eggs," said Adam to himself. He was breathing hard from the climb. "What else did I expect to find in a nest?"

"Any hungry, carnivorous dinos?" yelled Tuppence again. Adam leaned over the edge to reply, and felt his tummy lurch when he saw how high he had climbed.

"Ulp! Um, no – just eggs. The mum must be out getting food."

"Get back down then and we can try somewhere else," said Benji.

"Who made you king?" said Adam with a grin. He turned to carefully climb down the trunk again, but

froze when he heard a worrying noise.

Crr-ack!

"Uh-oh."

One of the eggs in the centre of the nest had begun to rock slightly and a small crack had appeared on it. Adam knew he had to get away, but he was transfixed. Suddenly the egg jumped and a long beak burst out of it.

"Adam? What's going on?" Tuppence called.

"It's hatching!" he called. "The dino's coming out!"

"Awww!" said Tuppence. "Is it cute?"

Adam watched as the pterosaur beak hammered its way through the shell until it could poke its head out. In front of him sat a sticky-looking dorygnathus.

Its eyes were red and its beak long and toothy. Its jaw couldn't seem to contain all its teeth, so it had a comical - yet terrifying - overbite with long, curved, sharp canines.

"No," said Adam. "Not at all."

Crr-ack!

Another egg rocked in its nest, and Adam watched as a second beak thrust through the shell.

"GET!"
"DOWN!"
"GET!"
"DOWN!" shouted the lycos, who sped around in circles with worry.

"It's okay, they're just babies!" said Adam. "They can't even hunt or kill yet!"

But the first dorygnathus turned its head to the sound of Adam's voice and looked at him questioningly.

"Ma…ma?" it managed to say.

Adam's face fell. *Drat.* He had heard about this – he should have realised!

"Mama?" said the second.

"No! Not me!" said Adam, scrambling backwards. "Mama's gone to get food – back soon!"

"Mama! Mama!" screamed the first dory. It didn't care what Adam said – he was its Mama now!

Adam finally lowered himself off the nest and picked his way carefully down the trunk.

"MAMA! MAMA!" screamed the two baby dorys. "MAAAMAAA!"

Benji looked up to the nest as Adam dropped down to the ground.

"What's all that about?" he asked.

"It's, er, called imprinting," said Adam, almost blushing. "When a baby pterosaur hatches, it thinks the first person it sees is…" He

trailed away.

"Is…?" prompted Tuppence.

"Its mum," said Adam.

Benji and Tuppence exchanged a look and then collapsed into a fit of laughter.

"You're their mum now!" laughed Benji. "Congratulations! You must be so proud!"

Adam tried to walk away, but the twins were laughing so hard they could not follow.

"MAMA!" came a deafening call from above.

"Aw, don't go Mummy!" teased Tuppence. "Just one more bedtime story?"

Adam shook his head and sighed.

"How do I get myself into these scrapes?" he muttered and pressed on through Pteratopolis.

*

"That's it, give me some slack!" called Chloe. She had taken the paracord and wrapped

it around herself to make a sort of harness. She tied the other end around a rock from the ground and weighed it up in her hand.

"Are you doing what I think you're doing?" asked Oska.

"Making a pulley? Yup…" said Chloe. She didn't even look over to Oska, her concentration fixed only on the canopy above her. "Here goes nothing…"

With a grunt, Chloe threw the rock with all her strength. It sailed upwards but fell short of the branch she was aiming for by some distance.

"…And that's the end of *that* plan!" she said.

"Hey, that's not the Bastion spirit!" said Dag, retrieving the rock. "Maybe we just need a bit of physics? Can I borrow your belt, Chloe?"

Chloe handed over the ragged cord holding her trousers up. Using a piece of fabric ripped from a backpack, Dag set about inventing. Chloe tried to stop herself from laughing – Dag always

made a strange face when he was concentrating; left eye squinted and tongue out to the side.

Within a minute or two, he was finished.

"There you go – a slingshot! Humans have used these for thousands of years. Go on, give it a spin!"

Chloe took it and felt the weight of it in her hand. Adding the rock with the paracord attached, she started to spin. And spin. And spin, until–

WHOOSH! She released the sling and the rock flew out of it, sailing upwards and over a protruding branch which jutted out from the top of the tree. The paracord ribboned through the air behind it like the tail of a kite.

"Remarkable!" said Oska.

Chloe gave Dag a celebratory fist-bump. Dag went to retrieve the rock on the end of the rope and nodded to Chloe.

"Dag, when you're ready: pull!"

Dag heaved on the length of paracord. The thin rope would have been difficult for a human to handle, but his thick scales and pointy claws made it easier for him to pull. As they had planned, Chloe rose into the air easily. She gave a small whoop of delight and waited for Dag to lift her up to the branch above. Below, Dag walked away from the tree with the cord over his shoulder. Again, any human would have broken into a sweat with all the lifting, but iguanodons were made of stronger stuff.

"Slow!" called Chloe. She was reaching the branch now and didn't want to arrive with a bump to the head from the fast approach. Nor did she want Dag to continue pulling once she reached the top, only to tip her balance and pull her straight back down to the ground with a sticky 'splat!'.

"WOAH!" she said as the branch came close. Dag halted and waited as she climbed on to the

branch. "Not bad," she muttered to herself. She balanced on top of the branch and teetered over to the large nest. "Kind of fun, actually..."

Coming to the edge of the nest, Chloe looked over to the other tall towers and came to the same conclusion Adam had; it must be hunting time, as all of the pterosaurs in Pteratopolis were nowhere to be seen.

Well, almost all...

Chloe reached the nest of sturdy branches and twigs and pulled herself over the top. She had to scramble to reach the lip of the construction and at one point her legs were left dangling in mid-air far above the ground below.

"Nearly... come on Chloe!" she grunted, spurring herself on. She pulled one last time and toppled into the nest. "Oof!"

Silence.

Chloe froze as she found herself with a nest full of armed dinosaurs, dressed in black and

staring straight at her. The four batrachognathuses seemed to be playing cards of some sort and looked more shocked than she did. Their short, stubby faces were formed into what Chloe would call an 'uh-oh' look – the kind that Adam used to wear back in Bastion when he kicked his ball and it ended up smashing a window in a greenhouse.

"Boss… it's an intruder!" whispered one of the guards to the other.

"I know!" he said. "I can see her!"

"So… what do we do?" asked the third batra.

All three looked at each other and shrugged. Chloe, still frozen to the spot, watched as one batra reached down slowly to his belt, where a weapon was strapped.

"GET HER!" he yelled.

Chloe found her feet finally and leapt up, out of the nest. She jumped off the edge onto the thick branch she had just balanced across. High

above the ground, she wobbled and saw Dag and Oska waiting below.

"DAG!" she yelled. "Take the strain!"

"What?" Dag replied. "*It's going to rain?*"

But he soon saw what she was planning. Having reached the end of the branch, she stood with her arms out like a high wire act. She knew that what she was about to do was pure lunacy…

"STOP INTRUDER!" came the call from the nest. The batras were clambering over the edge and waving a pulse blaster at Chloe. She had to get down – and she had chosen the quickest route possible.

Still attached to the harness, Chloe closed her eyes… and jumped.

"Good grief!" yelled Oska unhelpfully. Dag was caught by surprise. He saw the rope tighten and the rock with the end of the paracord attached whipped out of his claw. He yelped and ran after it.

141186_Dino Wars 2 J   ID: 2   B   data: 18-08-09   08:34:28   kolor: Black

Chloe felt the wind on her face as she fell. She trusted that Dag, her oldest friend, would have the strength to break her fall by pulling the rope tight. But below, Dag did not even have hold of the rope…

He raced forward, following the end of the cord and watched as Chloe plummeted towards the hard stone ground. Just metres away from the stone, he leapt – and grabbed it. He immediately stopped it from dragging across the ground and pulled tight.

Chloe felt the cord tighten and she opened her eyes. She was suspended just three metres from the ground, bouncing slightly as the cord took her weight – but she was safe.

She looked over to Dag and winked.

"Don't you ever, ever, EVER do that again!" said Dag, lowering her to the ground. He stepped forward and cut through the cord with his sharp claw. Chloe fell the last few feet to the

ground.

"I wasn't planning to!" she said. She got to her feet and pointed upwards. "Sorry. We've got company."

Chloe broke out into a run and Dag and Oska joined her. Above, the batra guards had taken to the sky and were circling above them, shouting warnings.

"STOP OR… OR, UM… WE'LL DO SOMETHING!" called one of the guards.

"OR WE'LL SHOOT!" said another. The city of Pteratopolis was obviously so inaccessible that the guards had never even seen an intruder before, let alone know what to do if they did. Chloe reflected as she ran that they were probably the first non-pterosaurs to ever set foot (or claw) inside the city walls.

Out of the corner of her eye she saw some other figures running forwards. She feared for a moment they were other batra guards, but

pterosaurs were slow on land and preferred to fly instead. The figures grew closer and she could see it was Adam and the twins, followed by the surprisingly fast lycorhinuses; Grak, Trek, Karp and Hart. Adam ran next to her.

"Is this your doing?" he said, breathless.

"Oh, shush!" said Chloe.

They ran as fast as they could, but neither had a clue where they were going. As they ran past a cliff, Adam suddenly spotted something.

"Look! A door!" he yelled. Sure enough, a set of dark wooden doors was fixed into the rock. "Head that way!"

"It's okay, I don't think the guards are very good at their job," said Chloe. "They seem to have given up and–"

PEW! PEW!

The sound of a pulse blaster rang out and the rock behind Chloe exploded into dust.

"Never mind! HEAD FOR THE DOORS!"

Chapter Five.

The doors were finely crafted out of dark oak and looked old and heavy. Adam recognised them as the sort that might have hung on a cathedral – he had seen pictures of the massive churches in books, but the buildings themselves had been destroyed many years before he was born, when the fighting and bombing of the Dino Wars were at their worst. As they skidded to a halt outside the doors, he was glad to have Dag and Oska – together stronger than any human – to help heave

them open.

PEW! PEW!

The pulse blasts from the guards flying above ricocheted off the wall above, sending dust scattering over them.

"Pull!" called Adam, his mouth full of rock dust.

"We are!" called Oska. With one final wrench, the doors opened and Adam ushered his friends inside. With a glance up to the hapless guards arguing amongst themselves, Adam ran into the dark space beyond the doors.

Inside it was pitch black and silent. Dag dragged the door closed and thankfully found a key in the lock. He turned it just in time to hear the unmistakable sound of a batra guard flying head-first into the thick wooden door.

They stood quietly for a moment. The only sound in the darkness was their breathless panting.

"So… now what?" said Tuppence.

Even in the gloom, Adam could tell that all eyes were turning towards him for an answer, like he had planned this all out in fine detail.

"Um… how about some light?" he said finally. "Dag, have you got anything?"

The sound of rummaging in backpacks came from Dag's direction and he piped up with:

"Ah-ha! Just the thing!"

A glow appeared in the dark as Dag pulled out the yellow Dilotron crystal from Bastion and the orange crystal they had recently taken from Raptor City. On their own they just let out a dim glow but when held together, they shone like stars.

"Brilliant, thanks Dag," said Adam. He looked around to see his crew looking tired and scared. He took the crystals and held them in one hand so the glow was at its brightest. He walked towards a dark passageway. It was wide enough for two people to walk side by side. Adam stepped forward into the shadows.

"This has been carved out of the rock," said Dag. "A man-made tunnel. Or dino-made, maybe…"

"Definitely human-made," said Oska. "The mountains of rubbish had to have pipes and tunnels fitted to allow any nasty gases to leak out safely. If they didn't, there was a chance that the gases released when the rubbish broke down would build up and cause an explosion."

"Makes sense," said Chloe. "So, are we safe? What if any 'nasty gases' are left?" Oska shook his head.

"This mountain is over a thousand years old so I think we should be alright. Also, humans would never have fitted such ornate doors. No, if you ask me, this has been re-used by the pterosaurs. Maybe as a–"

"A temple?" finished Adam.

The passageway had reached an end and led them into an open space. It was a cavern deep within the mountain with a tall ceiling and old miner's lamps providing light. No longer needed, Adam put the Dilotron crystals in his pockets. Spreading out in front of him were rows and rows of pterosaurs, knelt down on the ground.

Hundreds of them, thought Adam. *So this is why there was no one above ground. They were all in church!*

"Are they… praying?" asked Benji.

Thankfully he was quieter than normal and none of the dinosaurs moved. Adam held his finger to his lips and pointed at the far side of the cavern, where an ornate gold table was placed and in the centre of it sat an object similar to the crystals now stashed in his pocket. The crystal on the table however was glowing blue. Behind the table was the stone wall of the

temple, with a giant boulder in front of it. It was carved with the same beautiful designs as they had seen above ground.

"ALL RISE!" came a voice from the front. A pteranodon stood at an altar, a white hat with gold embroidery covering its head crest. It spread its wings out as the other pterosaurs seated on the ground raised their heads. Adam gulped when he saw the impressive size of the pteranodon's wingspan.

"I'm guessing he's in charge then," he said under his breath. His brain was racing – they were stuck in an underground temple with hundreds of pterosaurs. Looking over at them he could see all sorts of flying dinosaurs from massive quetzalcoatluses to tiny dimorphdons. The crystal they had come to claim was right in front of them. There was certainly nowhere to escape to at this point, so he had only one choice.

"Hello!" he called aloud in what he had meant to be a friendly tone of voice. Nerves got the better of him however and his voice wavered with fear. Dag and Chloe looked at him as if he had suddenly lost his mind.

A female preondactylus near to him turned and shrieked.

"Ahh!" she yelled. "A human!"

Similar shrieks followed. The shouts settled down to a murmur after a few seconds.

"Shh, shh, shh!" said the pteranodon priest. He clearly had control over his congregation as they were immediately silent. "Welcome, friend!" he said. "This is highly unusual, but please, come forward."

Adam froze for a second. He had suspected that the pterosaurs would not bring weapons to a temple and so he and his friends would be safe, but he really hadn't thought much beyond shouting 'hello'. Chloe poked him in the small of his back.

"Off you go then…"

He stumbled forwards down the aisle, rows of winged dinosaurs staring at him. He reached the front.

"I'm Adam," he said.

"D'Arpeth," said the priest. "You are trespassing in our city, Adam."

"Sorry about that. We're kind of on an important mission," he said. "And we need your help."

D'Arpeth seemed to smile (although it was hard to tell with a beaked dinosaur – his eyes definitely twinkled). He raised his wings out and spoke to the rest of his flock.

"He asks for forgiveness!" he said.

"Then he is forgiven!" said the crowd as one. "If he believes!"

"He asks for help!" D'Arpeth said.

"Then he shall receive!" said the crowd. "If

he believes!"

D'Arpeth turned to Adam.

"And do you believe, Adam?" he asked. "Do you believe in the power of the holy stone?" He looked over to the blue Dilotron crystal.

Adam smiled and pulled out the yellow and orange crystals from his pockets. They glowed even brighter now, close to the power of the blue crystal. The crowd of pterosaurs gasped when they saw.

"Oh yeah. I *definitely* believe…"

*

The hubbub in the temple had grown to a deafening level; the pterosaurs were chatting and gossiping about the strange humans and dinosaurs that had burst into their service,

brandishing what looked to be copies of the holy stone that they worshipped. D'Arpeth, his mouth hanging open with shock, shook his head in disbelief.

"But… but…" he stammered. "But there is only one holy stone…"

"'Fraid not pal," said Dag. "And we *may* have to borrow yours for a bit."

The dinosaurs on the front rows of the temple heard this and a new wave of murmurs spread throughout the grand hall.

"Keep your voice down!" commanded D'Arpeth. "I think you had better come with me."

He hopped to the side and opened a door in the rock wall. He nodded for them to get in. Adam did as he was told and the rest followed.

The door slammed behind them and Adam found himself in a vestry, a room to the side of the temple where D'Arpeth prepared for his services. Various embroidered fancy hats sat on hooks and a painted picture of D'Arpeth with the blue Dilotron crystal hung on the wall. Out in the temple, he could be heard telling his congregation to calm down and leave in an orderly manner.

"Maybe I should have held off asking to borrow the crystal?" said Dag. "Some of them seemed a bit upset…"

The door opened again and they were rejoined by D'Arpeth and a tall ornithodesmus.

"It looks like we have a lot to talk about," said D'Arpeth. He stood still long enough for the tall ornitho to take his hat off for him and hang it up. She then rushed over to pour him a glass of wine, which he gulped down.

"Of course," said Chloe. "Firstly, thank you for welcoming us. I know we weren't invited, but as you'll find out, we really are in a pickle."

D'Arpeth's eyes twinkled again.

"You know, good manners are so hard to find nowadays, don't you think?" he said. "What's your name, my dear?"

"Chloe," said Chloe. "This is Dag, Oska, Benji, Tuppence, and Grak, Trek, Karp and Hart."

D'Arpeth struggled to take in all the names.

"Quite the band of merry men, aren't you?" he said. "S'Ariah, fetch some refreshments for our guests while they tell me about themselves."

Adam breathed a sigh of relief and sat down at a table with D'Arpeth. It was such a welcome difference from their encounters in Raptor City!

While S'Ariah, the tall ornithodesmus, fetched drinks, Adam told them about Bastion. He told them how he found the secret, buried headquarters of the Allied Human Forces, and how he had accidentally set in motion the Coda Program. As D'Arpeth listened intently, he explained how, if they were to stop the process that could kill all the dinosaurs on New Earth, they would need four Dilotron crystals.

When he was finished, Adam sat back and stared anxiously at D'Arpeth. The pteranodon priest looked into his wine and swirled it around in the glass. The whole room was silent while they waited for his judgement.

"You *do* believe us, don't you?" said Dag, breaking the tension. D'Arpeth laughed.

"Yes, of course! This would have been a terrible amount of work just for a prank," he said. "The fact that you have two other crystals helps your case. May I see them?"

Adam placed the crystals on the table. D'Arpeth stared at them intently with a look Adam had seen before, in the crazed eyes of Stryker, the Raptor leader.

"They have the same aura," he said. He snapped his eyes away from them and Adam passed the crystals back to Dag, who stored them in one of his many pockets. "We worship our holy stone, you see."

"Makes sense," said Oska. "Dilotron crystals radiate a sort of power."

"We believe that our holy stone protects us and is the source of our strength as a species," said S'Ariah from the back of the room.

"We used ours to make the light bulbs work," shrugged Tuppence. "They're just glowy rocks really."

D'Arpeth looked up, seemingly offended by his 'holy stone' being called 'just a rock'. Chloe jumped in.

"But very dear, special rocks that obviously have a place in the heart of your city," she said. She didn't want the pterosaurs to think they wouldn't take care of the crystal if they were allowed to take it. "So… what do you think, D'Arpeth? Can we use your crystal to help save dino life on New Earth?"

Another long pause.

"My dear, if it were up to me you could take it straight away," he said eventually. "However I am but a simple priest. I need to consult our council of elders who run our city."

Adam nodded.

"Then please do so. We've got plenty of time!"

"Not really," said Dag, looking at his watch. "We've got little over two weeks to get the crystals and get to–Ow!"

Dag rubbed his leg where Chloe had kicked him.

"Shut up!" she hissed through her teeth. D'Arpeth stood and bowed his head to the group.

"As time is pressing, I will visit the elders immediately," he said. "S'Ariah, please feed our guests and keep them in the vestry. I fear the crowd outside may not take kindly to the idea of a group of strangers walking off with our holy stone."

He bowed again and left the room.

The group gathered around a large table in the vestry, Benji and Tuppence elbowing each other out of the way. They had not eaten a proper meal in days and their rations for the journey were meagre to start with. They all sat and waited politely.

"Can't wait!" said Tuppence.

"Me neither. These terror-whatsits seem pretty classy. Bet their food is ace!" said Benji.

"I've sent out for fresh food," said S'Ariah,

placing dishes in front of each guest. "It should be here very soon."

"Thank you – S'Ariah isn't it?" said Chloe.

"Yes ma'am," said S'Ariah, bowing.

"You don't need to bow to her!" said Adam with a laugh. "Or any of us. We're just a bunch of kids! Well, except for Oska over there."

S'Ariah smiled, but bowed out of habit.

"But you are our guests, so I will serve you in any way I can," she said. As she bent to lay the cutlery, Chloe whispered to her.

"So what's Pteratopolis like?"

"It's like… home. That's the only way to describe it! Of course, I've never even been off the mountain, so I wouldn't have anywhere else to compare it to."

Adam leaned in.

"You've never left Pteratopolis? But you can fly!"

"I'm just a novice. I can't leave the city until

I pass my tests," she said, looking around to see if there were any other pterosaurs listening. Making sure they weren't overheard, she whispered animatedly, "I can't wait! I should be asking you what the outside world is like! Is it amazing?"

Adam and Chloe exchanged a look. S'Ariah seemed so young and full of hope that it seemed cruel to tell her that beyond the mountain was just acres of scrubland where scavengers roamed. Or that every now and again there was a city of carnivorous dinosaurs waiting to eat you.

"Yeah. Amazing," said Chloe. S'Ariah smiled again and continued to set the table.

The door sprang open and in marched several tall pterosaurs. They walked to the side of each guest, their heads held high.

"Ah, perfect timing! Ladies and gentlemen… your dinner!" said S'Ariah. Benji and Tuppence looked around, curious as to where the plates of food were going to appear from; maybe they had them tucked under their wings? The pterosaurs each leaned forward and opened their beaks. After a few heaves and coughs, they each regurgitated a whole raw fish onto the plate, covered in a film of saliva.

"Freshly caught salmon from our hunting grounds! You're lucky, it's usually only the council of elders that get this special service," S'Ariah said.

Chloe and Adam looked down at the fish on their plate, the bright eyes still staring up at them.

"Regurgitated fish?" whispered Adam.

"To refuse it would be an insult," warned Chloe.

"After you then…"

Looking around, the rest of the group was

similarly horrified. Benji and Tuppence looked like they had just seen a major natural disaster flatten their home. Oska gulped and shrugged. He tucked in, ripping the flesh from the bones. The twins looked disgusted.

"What? I *am* a carnivore, after all," he said, his mouth full. "It's quite delicious. Adam, Chloe, your species has been eating raw fish for thousands of years. Your forefathers called it 'sushi'. So eat up!"

Adam hesitantly cut off a small chunk and placed it in his mouth. It was surprisingly acceptable.

Halfway through the meal, Dag made a show of cutting up his fish while also secretly eating a fruit bar he had stashed in a pocket. He leaned in and whispered to Adam, so that he could not be heard from the other the end of the table, where Oska was exchanging rude jokes with the twins and a blushing S'Ariah.

"Adam, I was meaning to tell you about earlier," he said. "When I was walking with Oska, he said some stuff."

"Stuff?" Adam said. His mouth was full of fish, which he was quite enjoying now.

"Yeah. He started talking about the Dino Wars. He seemed pretty bitter about the humans starting it."

Adam stopped chewing.

"Are you saying he's still anti-human?" Adam asked. Dag shrugged.

"Maybe. Just thought we should keep an eye on him."

"Dag, he helped us escape from Raptor City and chose to come with us. He abandoned his own species to help the mission," said Adam. "I'm sure he did some things in the war that we wouldn't agree with – everyone did. But he's one of us now."

Adam turned back to his meal, ending the

conversation. Dag glanced over to Oska, who smiled and raised his glass of wine with a wink.

After Adam and his crew of crystal hunters had finished their meal and Dag had chomped his way through a few fruit bars, D'Arpeth reappeared back through the door. He came in with his head bowed and his claws clasped in front of him. The room was immediately silent.

"Well?" said Chloe. "What was the verdict? Will the elders allow us to take the Dilotron crystal – um, I mean, holy stone?"

D'Arpeth was silent for a few more moments while the rest of the room held their breath, including S'Ariah.

"In principle, yes…" he said eventually.

"Yes! Get in!" said Benji.

"Woooo!" said Tuppence. There was a great exhale of breath and the room hummed with excitement again.

"Wait, wait!" said Adam, hushing his friends.

"What do you mean *in principle*? Sounds like there's a 'but'?"

"Well yes, naturally. The crystal, as you call it, is a holy relic to us. We could not allow you to take it away without some conditions."

Chloe laughed.

"Ah, yes I see! We completely understand, don't we?" she said. "I mean, we'll bring it straight back of course…"

"In all honesty, I expected the elders to laugh me out of the room. But it appears there is a prophecy," said D'Arpeth. He produced from under his wing a tattered scroll.

I wonder what else he's got up there? thought Adam.

"The Scroll of Fortune!" gasped S'Ariah. She bent down to whisper to Chloe. "It's our sacred writings. There are predictions of the future and rules about what must be done."

Unrolling it on the table, D'Arpeth began to read.

"*'And it is foreseen that into the home of the pterosaurs shall come a hero, ready to serve their kin and their world. And this hero shall take the holy stone for the greater good, after completing the trials.'*"

A hero! thought Adam. He had never thought of himself as a hero before, but now he thought about it, he had left his home in order to save the planet so he supposed that, yes, he was a hero! He felt pride welling in his belly. He felt taller somehow, his mood was–

"Wait a minute!" he said, interrupting his own train of thought. "What 'trials'?"

D'Arpeth looked down on the scroll, reading the tiny writing.

"Yes, it's quite clear. You will first have to prove your heroism by completing a series of tests. Then, and only then, you may take the crystal, having sworn to return with it."

Adam suddenly became aware of everyone looking at him. He looked back and tried to use his confident 'leader' voice.

"In that case... take me to the trials."

Chapter Six.

"I don't suppose that prophecy thing of yours tells you if we're going to actually save the planet or not, does it?" asked Dag. They were in another part of Pteratopolis – they had been moved from the temple and were now in a hut on the ground level that the pterosaurs had constructed to house their weaponry. It was a crude structure, built from logs and branches again but this time not in the style of a nest. They had built what Adam supposed was an armoury, with proper walls and a roof, but they were rickety to say the least. Adam thought that it was a good job Pteratopolis was inaccessible to enemies – their weapons would be easy to find and steal if any other soldiers did manage to make it through the city walls.

"It's, um, not mentioned," said S'Ariah apologetically. She had joined Dag and Adam on their trip to the armoury to help them pick out weaponry (and also to keep an eye on them – they were non-pterosaurs after all, and D'Arpeth had insisted that she stay with them to make sure they weren't planning to take over the city).

"Tsk," said Dag. "Pity. I could do with some good news."

"Do you think a shield is too much?" asked Adam. He was dressed in battle armour which the dinosaurs had looted from the humans they had defeated in the Dino Wars. He held up a plastic riot shield and looked

himself up and down in the mirror.

"Too much? You're not dressing for a ball, Adam. You're going to be tested on your strength and fighting ability," said Dag.

"I think a shield is an absolute *must*," said S'Ariah, picking out an axe for him. She passed it to him to test out for size. "After all, you never know what you might come up against in the labyrinth."

Adam span around to face her.

"The *what*?"

"The labyrinth of course. Where you will complete the trials. Hmm, maybe you're more of a sword kind of guy?" she asked, swapping the axe for a broadsword so heavy that Adam couldn't even lift it.

"S'Ariah, what labyrinth?" said Dag. "When they said trials, I thought they meant a demonstration or something."

"Oh no!" said S'Ariah. "It used to be the final

training for our knights. They had to enter the labyrinth, the network of tunnels that go under the mountain, and battle whatever horrible beasts and deadly traps that lie down there. Normally they had to retrieve their sword from the belly of the caves, but you'll be searching for the holy stone, of course."

Dag gulped.

"B-beasts?" he stammered.

"Traps?" said Adam. He suddenly wasn't so keen to be a hero after all. S'Ariah, oblivious to their trembling nerves, placed the broadsword back and gave Adam a small dagger to slip through his belt. "S'Ariah, how many knights have completed the labyrinth?"

S'Ariah thought for a moment.

"None so far," she said, matter-of-factly. "We had to scrap it. Now they just do a written test instead. So I guess you'd be the first to surviv-, um, I mean, complete it! Exciting, huh?"

Adam turned white with worry.

"Move over boys! Chlo' is gonna glow!" came a call from outside the hut. It was Tuppence of course, followed by Chloe.

"What are you doing? You should be getting some rest," said Adam. "Getting ready to cheer me on!"

Chloe didn't even crack a smile.

"Adam, I've been thinking. I'm going to take the trials instead," she said. Adam couldn't help but let out a loud barking laugh, then stopped as her disapproving glance fell on him. "Why not? I'm fast, I'm clever…"

"You can't be the hero of the prophecy, Chloe, think about it–"

"Because I'm a girl?" said Chloe.

"No! I never said that!" said Adam. "You're just a kid!"

"So are you!"

Chloe and Adam found themselves head to

head again. Adam was turning red with rage, while Chloe was breathing deeply through her nostrils like a bull.

"Ooh! How exciting!" said the always jolly S'Ariah. "Looks to me like you both have the temperament of a hero. In my experience, they're all a bit hot-headed. Sorry, that was meant to be a compliment…"

Adam turned away from her and took off his armour. Dag went to help his friend and whispered in his ear.

"Adam, think about this; if Chloe goes into the labyrinth as well as you, it doubles our chances of getting the crystal," said Dag. "It doesn't matter who the 'hero' is, as long as we get the crystal and get out of here."

Adam knew he was right. He was always right. He hated him at that moment for being right, even though he was his best friend in the entire world. Adam turned back to S'Ariah.

"Is there any reason why both of us can't go in the labyrinth at the same time?" he asked. S'Ariah looked flustered, her scaly skin glowing as she thought.

"Um… um… no! I don't think so?" she said finally. Adam nodded and turned to Chloe.

"If you go in there, we go our separate ways," he said. "It's the only way we won't annoy each other and will mean we can find the crystal quicker."

"Agreed," said Chloe.

"If you go in there, I can't look out for you," he said.

"I should hope not!" Chloe laughed. "You don't need to!"

Adam smiled and shook his head.

"Of course I do… you're my little sister!"

They exchanged an awkward handshake.

"Aw! It must be lovely having a brother or sister!" said S'Ariah. Chloe rolled her eyes.

"Or… not? Maybe not, then? Never mind…"

There was still one night to spend in Pteratopolis before Adam and Chloe could start the trials, so Adam placed his armour and weaponry down and made to leave the armoury hut with Dag. Chloe stayed to try on her own armour and weapons, assisted by S'Ariah and the ever-helpful Tuppence, who was playing with a spear. As Adam left to get some rest in their guest-nest, he whispered to S'Ariah.

"Good night. Make sure you tell Chloe about the horrible beasts and deadly traps, won't you? It's only fair that she knows all the details…"

*

Adam woke to the sound of screaming. He leapt up, instantly awake, and looked for whatever disaster was going on that was causing the racket. Seeing his friends asleep around him and only just starting to stir, he relaxed. Sticking his head out of the guest-nest, he heard the sound more clearly. It was the call of the pterosaurs; each morning they saluted the sunrise with a deep squawking, like a cockerel crowing.

He was surprised he had slept at all. Today was the day he entered the labyrinth ready to face whatever horrors that lurked inside. He had spent the first part of the night fretting and fidgeting, worrying about what he would come up against, but then exhaustion took over and he slept soundly for hours. The nest was extraordinarily comfortable, lined with moss and feathers.

"Dag, wake up," said Adam, nudging his friend.

"Hmm?" mumbled Dag, half-asleep. "I don't wanna go to school…"

Eventually he woke and stretched up high. The rest of them started to stir and Chloe stood.

She looked as scared as Adam.

"You don't have to do this, you know," he said. Chloe shook her head.

"I know. But I want to," she said. "I want to help with the mission. Let's get on with it."

They ate breakfast which was, unsurprisingly, more raw fish. Adam was too nervous to eat, but the hunters who had caught the food stood by the side of their table. Adam faked enthusiasm, eating a little, but wrapping the rest in a napkin and shoving it in a pocket when they weren't looking. Adam and Chloe then went to the armoury and dressed with the help of Dag and Tuppence. They picked their weapons and walked silently to the temple, led by S'Ariah, who was as chirpy as always.

"Sleep well?" she asked. "No nightmares of labyrinth monsters? Ah, good…"

She knocked three times on the large wooden doors of the temple and then opened them, ushering everyone inside. Stepping forward, Adam and Chloe walked through the tunnel and found themselves in the temple again, deep in the trash mountain.

"Welcome, adventurers!" said the booming voice of D'Arpeth. He stood at the front of the temple, in front of the golden table. Adam noted that the blue Dilotron crystal, their 'holy stone', was gone - taken into the labyrinth and hidden. Sat behind the altar were five pterodactyls. They had greying scales and were peculiarly fat - it was a strange sight to see the usually thin and lithe dinosaurs with pot-bellies.

These must be the council of elders, thought

Adam. *Looks like they get the first pick of the fresh fish at mealtimes.*

D'Arpeth beckoned them forwards and presented them to the ancient dinosaurs.

"My lords and ladies, I present the challengers: Adam and Chloe Caine."

The largest of the pterodactyls leaned forward to see them better.

"Children?" he said, his voice weak with age. "This is no place for children!"

"Don't let our age fool you, my lord!" said Adam. "We are the finest our city has to offer."

"Certainly the stupidest…" muttered Chloe under her breath.

The elder's eyes lingered on them a moment longer, then he seemed to shrug.

"Very well. If the trial is to begin, then guards, please take the deposit," he said, waving a wrinkled claw at the shadows of the temple. Marching out of the shade came ten batra guards, all wielding pulse blasters. Chloe recognised the three she had run from just the previous day. They walked down the aisles of the temple with a threatening 'stomp-stomp-stomp' until they came to a halt beside Benji and Tuppence.

"Mornin'," said Benji to the nearest. "What d'you want?"

Without a word, the guard grabbed Benji's wrist and twisted it behind his back, clipping it to his other arm with handcuffs.

"Ow! Oy! Leave off! Tupps – tell 'im!" shouted Benji. But Tuppence was shouting also as another guard handcuffed her.

"Leave them alone!" called Chloe. "What is the meaning of this?"

D'Arpeth looked sheepish.

"Ah, yes. There is something I neglected to tell you…" he said. "The elders insisted on some sort of insurance. The tunnels lead all over the

mountain you see – if you were to find the holy stone, you could just escape – we want to make sure you come back here."

The lycos ran around the legs of the guards, shouting and hissing at them. Trek and Karp pecked at their shins, and the huge guards let out a high-pitched scream.

"LET!"
"GO!"
"LET!"
"GO!" the lycos yelled in turn.

Adam was turning red with rage.

"That was not the deal!" he said, almost shouting. Chloe laid a hand on his arm to tell him to calm down. "What if we take the crystal away from Pteratopolis? What will you do then?"

"We will take the children as our slaves!" said the head elder. "Until you return with our holy stone."

"NO!" said Chloe. It was her turn to lose her temper. "That's out of the question!"

Oska came to her and whispered in her ear.

"Go, my dear! I will look after the children," he said. "Fret not!"

Something about his tone made Chloe trust him. She looked to the twins, who also nodded at them to go ahead.

"We'll be alright! There isn't a lock on New Earth I can't pick!" said Tuppence. "Although this is *really* tight… Loosen it a bit, will you mate?"

Chloe and Adam faced the elders again.

"Are you ready?" asked D'Arpeth. They nodded, too nervous to speak. "Then we will begin."

The eldest elder stood with the help of a cane and spoke with an deep, rough voice:

"Enter the labyrinth!" he boomed. "Behold

its secrets! Retrieve the holy stone! Only the true hero will succeed!"

Five of the batra guards stepped forward and walked to the back of the temple where the giant stone was up against the rock wall. With a large amount of grunting and groaning, they heaved the stone away from the wall to show a deep tunnel in the rockface. Adam and Chloe stepped forward and were handed miner's lamps by the guards. Peering into the dark of the labyrinth, Adam took his lamp gratefully.

"Still want to do this?" asked Adam.

"Yep," said Chloe. "You?"

"Of course," he lied. He really felt like running back to the nest and curling up in a ball. But that's why he was a hero, he told himself – he was facing his fear and doing it anyway. Dag stepped up to them and grabbed them both in a tight hug.

"Come back to us, alright?" he said. "Don't

take any risks. Just get in and out and come back safe."

Shaking, Adam swallowed and nodded.

"Let's go."

They stepped forward into the dark, and into the unknown.

Chapter Seven.

It wasn't long before they reached the first fork in the tunnels.

"Here we go then," said Adam. "You go that way, I'll go this way."

Chloe hesitated. She wanted to ask if splitting up was the right way to win the crystal, but she did not want to sound afraid in front of her brother. She chewed on her lip for a moment, then nodded.

"Okay. See you back at the temple," she said, forcing a smile. "Unless…"

Unless the horrors of the labyrinth get us first? thought Adam. *Yeah, I was thinking the same thing.*

"See you at the temple," he said. He turned and walked away. He too did not want to show his sister how scared he was. It was better to just get on with the trial and concentrate on staying alive.

The tunnels were winding and small. He was not used to squeezing through tiny gaps and found his breathing got heavier. He tried not to panic. He was used to the wide open spaces of Bastion and the scrublands beyond. Being underground felt unnatural.

He saw a light up ahead of him and laughed. The tunnels must loop back onto each other and Chloe was now heading towards him. He got closer and was about to speak when he realised that it was not his sister.

The figure in front of him was taller than Chloe and broader shouldered. Adam could not see a face in front of him as the light from the person's lamp was shining back at him, silhouetting the figure. Could this be the challenge? Another challenger to battle? Adam stopped and so did the figure.

"Hello?" he said, but the other person said nothing. Adam's own words echoed in the chamber. "Come forward!"

But the figure did nothing. Adam decided the time for action had come. He placed down his lamp and drew his dagger, running forward.

There was a crash as he ran headfirst into his own reflection.

Mirrors, thought Adam, rubbing his head where he had bumped it. *I can't believe I fell for that one. Stupid, stupid Adam!*

Looking further down the tunnel, the corners were highly polished until you could see your reflection in them, as Adam had done. It was a simple trick but an effective one, to confuse and disorientate the challenger.

Walking forwards, Adam had to stretch his arms out in front of him to stop himself from walking into another wall. He could no longer trust what he saw.

Stumbling ahead, he waved his lamp in front of him for light. The ground underfoot was getting damp and he realised that he could see his breath in front of him - the temperature had dropped. The tunnels were silent apart from his own footprints and the air was putrid; a thousand years of rotting trash was all around him.

"I must remember never to come here on holiday," he muttered to himself. He was trying to remain positive, but the fact was that he was deep underground, in the dark, with no idea where he was going. And it *stank*.

Just then his damp footsteps turned from a light 'squelch' into a definite 'splash'.

A puddle, he thought. *No matter.*

But the next step proved to be damper still

when he fell feet first into a freezing cold plunge pool. It was deep; he went straight in and the icy water covered his head and his helmet. His lantern sank to the bottom, extinguishing the light from all around him. It was such a shock that he hadn't had time to try to grab hold of the sides and the cold seemed to draw the breath from him instantly. In total darkness, he kicked until he reached the surface and caught a lungful of air, but the weight of his armour dragged him down again. He felt the panic building up inside him and he allowed himself to thrash and scream – but only for a second. Panic, if not handled correctly, can be deadly. Adam got the scream out of his system and then began to think clearly. He needed to get out of his armour if he wanted to live, otherwise the weight of it would drown him.

He wriggled and kicked until his breastplate came off and ripped at the fastenings covering

his legs. Finally he ripped off his helmet and found he was able to kick himself upwards again. He gasped for air and found the sides of the pool, heaving himself up.

He sat, dripping wet and shivering. He wanted to give himself a minute but knew that he had to get moving, to get his blood circulating again. He stood and pressed on, forcing his frozen limbs to move. The tunnels were now pitch black, his lamp having sunk to the bottom of the pool, but as he walked his foot clunked against a metal tin on the ground. Bending, he found what felt like an old ammunition box from the Dino Wars. His father had used them as all-purpose containers, cleaning them out and storing all sorts of items, from tools to rice. He unfastened the lid and felt inside. There were smooth plastic tubes inside. On a hunch, Adam snapped one and he was pleased to see a red light come from it.

Glow sticks, thought Adam. *The pterosaurs that built the pool of water knew that any lamp would perish, but still wanted to provide a sporting chance. So they left glow sticks to light the rest of the way. How thoughtful.*

Walking on, he came to an open cavern. It was nowhere near as large as the temple he had left behind, but at least there was room to stretch his arms around. He was still freezing, so he exercised to get warm. He noticed as he did some star jumps that the cavern had two exits. Each looked as dark and uninviting as the other, so his only choice was either left or right – one could lead to the Dilotron crystal, but it could also lead to certain doom. He chose the right-hand side exit and stepped forward to go through it.

Ding-a-ling-a-ling!

What was *that*? Of all the horrors and obstacles he expected to find in the labyrinth, a small child's bell was not one of them. He looked down to see that he had walked into a tripwire, which had been rigged up to make a bell ring above him. Suddenly he heard the sound of rustling in the dark.

"Crrk?" came the sound from the shadows.

"Hello?" said Adam. He cautiously walked forwards. In the gloom he saw two tiny, beady eyes shine in the light from his glow stick. "What are you then?"

"Crrk!" said the creature. Adam beckoned it closer.

"Come on, I won't hurt you!"

The small dinosaur, only as big as a chicken, or even the smallest of the lycorhinuses, stepped forward. It was thin and harmless looking, with only a sharp beak to boast as its weapon.

Adam recognised it as a parvicursor – his dad had made him memorise lots of dinosaurs from a book when he was young so he could know their weaknesses and defend himself if ever the Dino Wars were to return. He knew that although carnivorous, the parvicursor only ate ants and termites. They were also amazingly stupid; when they were brought back to life from extinction in the Dino Wars, scientists had been unable to make their brains any bigger. The result was that they couldn't speak at all, not even in single words like the lycos. Adam figured he was pretty safe with the little guy.

"What are you doing down here? When they said it was full of horrors, it wasn't you I had in mind!" he said. The parvicursor looked on, smacking its beak together. "Hungry? I don't think I can help I'm afraid…"

Adam trailed off as he glimpsed more twinkling of beady eyes in the darkness of the labyrinth.

Out of the darkness stepped not one, not two, but twenty other parvicursors. They each looked at Adam with a curious expression, tilting their heads like a quizzical dog.

"Crrk?" said one.

"Crrk! Crrk!" chanted another.

They want food, thought Adam. *And I'm it.*

He figured it out quickly; the pterosaurs kept a flock of parvis in their tunnels. Whenever they fed them, they would ring the bell so that when the challenger tripped the wire and rang the bell, the tiny dinosaurs would think it was lunchtime and come for him. The flock of parvicursors stepped closer, staring at Adam, their meal. It wasn't the termites they were used to, but they were too hungry to care – if it had meat on it, it would do.

Adam backed up, ringing the bell again by

accident as he stepped on the tripwire. This did nothing to help; even more parvicursors came running. Adam imagined how being pecked to death by thirty or so chickens would be and decided he didn't want to find out.

"CRRK! CRRK! CRRK!" shouted one of the dinosaurs. "CRRK! CRRK! CRRK!" Adam took this to mean: 'What are we waiting for? Let's eat him!' as the few dinosaurs at the front of the flock zipped forward and pecked him on the shins.

"Ow!" said Adam. The attack was small but brutal. Without his armour he was exposed and the dinosaur had drawn blood. "Get off!"

Another pecked and Adam yelled again. One went to nip his ankles but he dodged it. He leapt up onto a rock, the dinosaurs pecking at his feet. He was on the brink of panic again, but thankfully his memory kicked in and he reached down to his pocket.

"You want food? Here!"

He pulled out the fresh fish he had been given for breakfast from his pocket and unwrapped it. The parvicursors looked eager to try this new food, especially as it didn't look like it would put up a fight. Adam threw it behind him and closed his eyes.

He did not feel a rush of dinosaurs coming to peck him, but instead a surge of them as they pushed past him to get to the hunk of fish. With a sigh of relief, Adam ran on through the right-hand passage.

119

Chapter Eight.

The chamber was dark, lit only by a blue light from the centre, where the Dilotron crystal lay on a plinth. It was surrounded by grey, stone tiles on the floor, and the walls of the room were corrugated iron. As Adam entered with his glow stick, he cast a red ray of light into the room. He walked in carefully, looking for traps and tripwires in the gloom.

"Finally!" he said aloud on seeing the crystal. "Am I glad to see you!"

"Talking to yourself?" came a voice from the shadows. "First sign of madness, you know."

"Chloe?"

Chloe stepped out of the shadows and relit her miner's lamp, casting light into the chamber. She was still wearing her armour and, apart from being a bit mucky, looked relatively unscathed.

"Yikes! What happened to you?" she asked. "Where's your armour?"

Adam waved her away with his hand, exhausted.

"Never mind..." he said. "So, what's the trap here?"

"Good question," said Chloe, pacing around the room but keeping close to the wall. "I've been here a while but can't see anything. There must be *something*. The dinos wouldn't make it so we could just grab the crystal... would they?"

Adam found himself hoping that they might. He was wet, cold, tired and bleeding from the pecks on his legs. He eyed the crystal suspiciously.

"There's only one way to find out," he

muttered. He stepped forward. His foot fell onto one of the grey hexagonal tiles around the plinth. It immediately started to sink into the floor and a clank of chains began to echo around the chamber.

"Adam, move!" Chloe shouted. Adam looked up to see a steel cage above him, dropping fast. He leapt back, crashing against the wall. The sound of chains moving stopped, then started again slowly as whatever mechanism had been put in place by the pterosaurs winched the cage back up into the ceiling.

"Gah!" shouted Adam in frustration. "I could have had it if I was quicker!" He stood again and jumped up and down, preparing himself.

"What are you doing?" asked Chloe. "You're not trying again are you?"

"Of course," said Adam. "Now I know what's going to happen, I can get ready for it. I can roll out of the way of the falling cage."

Chloe laughed.

"Didn't you see it? It was made of iron! It's so heavy it'll chop off a leg if you don't roll out of the way in time."

Adam paused. His cheeks turned red.

She's right, he thought. *I hate it when she's right. And if she laughs at me again I'll...*

"You'd be no good to the mission with one leg!" Chloe continued to laugh.

"You do it then!" shouted Adam. "You wanted to find the crystal, be the hero; do it!"

"Fine, I will!"

Chloe stepped forward onto one of the grey tiles and the familiar clanking of chains began to sound. To Adam's astonishment, she did not attempt a commando-style duck and roll. Instead, she stood still and let the iron cage fall on top of her.

"Chloe!" Adam screamed. He was about to run to her when she turned and held up her hand.

"NO! Stop!" she said. Shocked, Adam did as he was told. "Don't you see? If the cage is on me, it means it can't fall on you."

Adam was lost for words.

"You mean…"

"You have to get the crystal, Adam," said Chloe. "You'll make a great hero. You've always had it in you."

Adam stood for a moment, staring at his sister in the cage. She had sacrificed herself, her safety, and the chance to become the hero of this part of their journey, and it was all for him.

"Wow. Thanks Chlo'."

Chloe smiled.

"Now get on with it," she said, being her normal, bossy self again. "I really want to get out of this trash mountain. It stinks like your socks after dinoball practice."

Again Adam did as he was told and stepped forward onto the tiles.

"Yes, *your Highness*! I shall do as I am–"

But the whirring and the clanking started again. Adam looked up and saw the gears and chains spinning in the ceiling, and an iron cage falling directly on top of him.

Chapter Nine.

CLANG!

The echo rang out through the chamber as the cage landed on the tiled floor. Adam, who had covered his head as a reflex action, took his arms away and looked up. Trapped.

"Two cages," said Chloe. Adam looked over to see a sheepish grin on her face. "Oops. Who knew?"

Adrenaline ran through Adam's veins and made him shake.

"You… you… YOU AND YOUR STUPID PLANS!" he yelled. "YOU HAD TO TRY AND BE CLEVER, DIDN'T YOU?"

"DON'T HAVE A GO AT ME! I WAS TRYING TO GET THE CRYSTAL!"

"BUT WE DON'T HAVE IT, DO WE?" Adam mocked. "NOW WE'RE STUCK LIKE A COUPLE OF–"

"SHHH!" said Chloe, putting her hands up as a sign of surrender.

"Don't shush me! I'll make as much noise as I–"

"SHHHHHH!"

Adam obeyed this time but only because all the shouting was making his throat hoarse. When he was finally quiet and the sound of his own heartbeat pumping in his ears had dimmed, he began to hear what Chloe had silenced him for.

A grinding, grating sound. The sound of a far off engine. It was coming from the ceiling above them and Adam knew he had heard it somewhere before. It was the sound of–

"DAG!" said Adam and Chloe together.

A rumble in the chamber told them they were right. The room rocked and shook. The Dilotron crystal vibrated on its plinth. It seemed as though the whole mountain was shaking, and then-

CRASH!

The ceiling caved in, rocks and ancient rubbish falling on their heads – though Chloe and Adam were nicely protected from falling debris by the roof of the cage – and then a large iguanodon with a set of razor-sharp rotating blades fell from the sky and landed neatly next to the Dilotron crystal. He hit a button to kill the engine and the blades of his heli-kit slowed to a stop.

"Yes!" said Dag, picking up the crystal. He looked up and saw Adam and Chloe for the first time. "Oh, alright guys?"

"Dag, what are you doing here?" asked Adam, relieved to see his friend.

"Well I thought, if you two are searching for this, there's no reason I can't try as well!" he smiled. "And I thought – 'Who needs to follow tunnels, when I can dig my own?'"

Chloe clapped.

"Brilliant! But how did you find us?" she asked.

"Easy!" Dag said, and brought out the two Dilotron crystals, which glowed orange and red against the remaining walls of the chamber. "These things glow whenever they are together. So I just let the crystals guide me – if it glowed stronger, that's where I went. Took about twenty minutes…"

Adam, exhausted and hysterical, let out a laugh that went on for far too long.

"Where would we be without you, Dag?" he said finally.

"Under a mountain in a couple of cages, apparently," shrugged Dag. "Now hold still. I've got something that will cut through those bars..."

*

Benji and Tuppence broke free from their guards to run and hug their friends as they emerged from the labyrinth. Even Oska high-fived the lycos in celebration.

Adam and Chloe were dusty, sweaty, tired and grumpy, but they still walked into the temple as though they had just won a battle. Dag walked between them and they each held up a crystal like trophy winners.

"Woooo!" yelled Tuppence.

"We got it! We got it!" sang Benji, with a little made-up dance.

Adam saw D'Arpeth and the council of elders sitting at the front of the temple. The elders did not look too pleased to see them, but D'Arpeth had a twinkle in his eye – if Adam didn't know any better, he would have said it was pride.

"Warriors! Challengers! Come hither!" D'Arpeth called. The three of them came to face him and knelt down on his order. "You have survived the labyrinth!"

"And I added a few more tunnels for you," said Dag.

"Who here is the hero who claims the holy stone for their mission?" said D'Arpeth, his wings spread for maximum effect.

Chloe nudged Dag.

"Hmm? Ah, well it was a team effort really..." Dag said, blushing. Adam shook his

head.

"Him. He does," he said. "Dag's the hero."

D'Arpeth looked surprised, but continued his grand speech.

"Then you must take it and carry on with your mission," he said. "But you must return it at the earliest opportunity!"

"We will," said Chloe. "And thank you."

There was a mumbling amongst the council of elders. The eldest stood, his hand on his cane shaking.

"We have a condition!" he announced.

"What now?" said Adam. He half-expected

them to add another trial, like jumping off the mountain or juggling fire.

"Forgive us, but the memory of the Dino Wars runs deep. Some of us cannot bring ourselves to trust humans, or other dinosaurs for that matter, completely. For that reason, I propose that a guardian from the pterosaur community is assigned to your group. To assure us that the holy stone will be kept safe, and brought back."

Chloe thought about it and grinned.

"Alright!" she said. "But we get to pick who comes along!"

Chapter Ten.

"Waaah-haaah!" screamed S'Ariah from high above the mountain path. "This is amazing! Wooooo!"

She circled and swooped in the sky, catching air currents and soaring around the group down below.

"Is she going to be like that the whole journey?" asked Adam. Chloe playfully hit him on the arm.

"Give her a break! It's the first time she's been allowed out of Pteratopolis. It's all new to her," she said. "Anyway, I'm sure the novelty will wear off soon."

Adam and Chloe walked in silence for a while, picking their way down the mountain path.

"That was pretty cool, insisting S'Ariah come with us," he said eventually. "And back in the chamber. Putting yourself in the cage like that – that took guts."

Chloe smiled.

"Pity it didn't work out like I planned," she said with a laugh.

"No, but still, you were a proper hero – thinking like a team instead of on your own."

Silence again. Then:

"You were always looking after me in Bastion. And Dag. And Benji and Tuppence. You're a hero too, Adam," said Chloe.

Adam put his arm around his sister and promised himself that whenever he felt the anger rising in him again, whenever the red mist of rage appeared in front of his eyes, he would think of this moment and remind himself that however much his sister and friends annoyed him – they were family.

"Hey everyone! How about a sing-song?" called Chloe.

"Yay!" cheered the twins.

"No!" Adam called. But it was too late.

"*Ninety-nine green bottles, hanging on a wall... Ninety-nine green bottles, hanging on a waaaaall...!*"

Chloe giggled as Adam groaned.

"How far to the next stop?" he moaned.

Chloe took a look at the map.

"Four days. Get used to it!"

Adam sighed.

"Fine. But I get to pick the next song!"

And the band of friends wound their way down the slope of the mountain, marching on to another adventure.

Dino Wars will return with

The Gladiator Games

Turn over for a sneaky preview!

"Where to, boss?" said Tuppence. Adam continued to stare at the map, befuddled.

"It's no good," he muttered. "This map is broken," he said. He looked up with a frown and an 'ah-well' shrug.

Chloe bent down and turned the map upside-down, until the points on the map reflected the cities on the horizon.

"Ah! Yes! I was... just, um, testing..." spluttered Adam. Chloe covered her mouth to stop herself from laughing while Dag bit on his claw. The others found something interesting to look at in the nearby wildlife (of which there was none). Adam did his best to carry on.

"So, going east to west, we have the Realm of the Giganotosaurus," He pointed to the industrial chimney, "then the Valley of the Ornithopods," He pointed to the simple bamboo-walled settlement. "Or Rextopia," he said, gesturing to the high stone walls.

"The question is: which do we fancy our chances with?" asked Chloe.

The team looked at each other.

"Well, the T-Rex place sounds a bit bitey-bitey," said Benji.

"And the Giganotosaurus place sounds a tad stompy-stompy?" chanced Dag.

"Ornithopods it is then!" said Adam. He clapped and rubbed his hands together. "A nice, friendly species. Should be a walk in the park."

"Finally!" said Chloe. "I don't know about you, but I don't fancy any quest, challenges or trials again any time soon."

"Exactly!" said Adam, laughing. "And thank goodness we don't have to meet any T-Rexes! I mean, I like an adventure, but I like my head too!"

The group laughed and prepared to set off again. Chloe, for one, found it refreshing that they were going to request a crystal from a friendly species of dinosaur. Maybe she could use politeness and flattery to ask for the crystal? Maybe she could be of use after all?

They were just about to take the first footstep

of many towards the Valley of the Ornithopods, when a loud rumbling sound piped up. It was deep, like an avalanche of rocks falling down a mountainside. Adam and Chloe exchanged worried looks.

"Dag, is that your tummy?" asked Oska.

"Not this time," said Dag. "S'Ariah, can you get an aerial view?"

The clumsy pterosaur nodded and spread her wings, unfurling her massive wingspan. She took a few steps and caught the wind, rising up quickly and swooping in circles until she found a thermal to hover on.

"Anything?" shouted Chloe. S'Ariah started to shout, but she was too far up for the team to hear. "What? Come lower!"

S'Ariah closed her wings, causing her to plummet towards the ground. She spread them again at the last second to slow her descent like a parachute. She landed next to Adam.

"I said: 'TROODONS! RUN!'"